USBORNE FIRST READING
Level One

USBORNE FIRST READING

The
**Three
Wishes**

Retold by Lesley Sims
Illustrated by Elisa Squillace

A Just So Story by Rudyard Kipling

How the
Elephant
got his **Trunk**

Illustrated by John Joven
Retold by Anna Milbourne

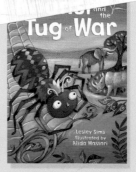

and the
Tug of **War**

Lesley Sims
Illustrated by
Alida Massari

USBORNE FIRST READING

**Old MacDonald
had a farm**

Illustrated by Pera Mantle

A Just So Story by Rudyard Kipling

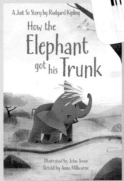

How the
Rhino
got his **Skin**

Illustrated by John Joven
Retold by Rosie Dickins

USBORNE FIRST READING

The
Ant
and the
Grasshopper

Retold by
Katie Daynes
Illustrated by
Marsel Eyckerman

A Just So Story by Rudyard Kipling

Why the
Kangaroo
Jumps

Illustrated by John Joven
Retold by Rob Lloyd Jones

USBORNE FIRST READING

The Lion and
the **Mouse**

Retold by
Mairi Mackinnon

A Just So Story by Rudyard Kipling

How the
Leopard
got his **Spots**

Illustrated by John Joven
Retold by Rosie Dickins

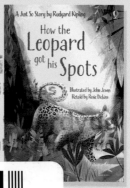

How the Crab got his Claws

by Rudyard Kipling

Illustrated by John Joven

Retold by Rosie Dickins

Reading consultant: Alison Kelly

Once, Crab was huge and he had no claws.

This story tells how
that changed.

In the beginning

the Wise Man told the animals how to behave.

He told every animal.

Crab ran away.

The other animals
played nicely.

Crab did NOT...

When Crab played,
the sea flooded...

SPLASH!

or turned to mud!

"WHO is doing that?"
asked the Wise Man.

"Not us," said
the animals.

"What about Crab?"
said a girl.

"He ran away
when you were
talking."

"Crab," called the
Wise Man. "Stop
playing with the sea!"

"Ha, ha. NO!"
shouted Crab.

"I'll do magic," warned the Wise Man.

Crab didn't care.

"I'm so small!" wailed Crab. "How will I eat?"

"I'll give you my scissors," said the girl.

"Then you can crack shells and eat nuts."

Crab took them.

Now *all* crabs have scissor-claws — and some really do eat nuts.

PUZZLES

Puzzle 1

Complete the sentence.

_____ did what he wanted.

Cow

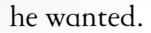

Turtle

Crab

Puzzle 2

Put the pictures in order.

A

The Wise Man did magic.

B

Crab shrank.

C

Crab was very big.

Puzzle 3

True or False?

Crab ran away.

Crab played nicely.

Crab got bigger.

Puzzle 4

Spot five differences
between the two pictures.

Answers to puzzles

Puzzle 1

<u>Crab</u> did what he wanted.

Puzzle 2

C — Crab was very big.

A — The Wise Man did magic.

B — Crab shrank.

Puzzle 3

Crab
ran away.
<u>True</u>

Crab played
nicely.
<u>False</u>

Crab got bigger.
<u>False</u>

Puzzle 4

About the story

This story is from the book *Just So Stories* by Rudyard Kipling, which tells how animals came to be the way they are.

Designed by Laura Nelson Norris
Series designer: Russell Punter
Series editor: Lesley Sims

USBORNE FIRST READING
Level Two

USBORNE FIRST READING

Farmyard Tales
The Snow Storm

Illustrated by
Stephen Cartwright

Usborne First Reading

Little Miss Muffet

Retold by Russell Punter
Illustrated by Lorena Alvarez

USBORNE FIRST READING

How Bear Lost his Tail

Retold by Lucy Bowman
Illustrated by Ciaran Duffy

Usborne First Reading

Doctor Foster
went to Gloucester

Retold by Russell Punter
Illustrated by David Semple

USBORNE FIRST READING

There Was A Crooked Man

Retold by Russell Punter
Illustrated by David Semple

USBORNE FIRST READING

Farmyard Tales
Barn on Fire

Illustrated by
Stephen Cartwright

Usborne First Reading

The **Dragon** and the **Phoenix**

Retold by Lesley Sims
Illustrated by Graham Philpot

USBORNE FIRST READING

Farmyard Tales
Surprise Visitors

Illustrated by
Stephen Cartwright

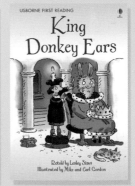

USBORNE FIRST READING

King Donkey Ears

Retold by Lesley Sims
Illustrated by Mike and Carl Gordon